To Sarah

Henry Holt and Company, *Publishers since 1866*
Henry Holt® is a registered trademark of Macmillan Publishing Group, LLC
175 Fifth Avenue, New York, NY 10010 · mackids.com

Library of Congress Cataloging-in-Publication Data
Names: Auerbach, Adam, author, illustrator. | Title: The Three Vikings / Adam Auerbach.
Description: First edition. | New York : Henry Holt and Company, 2019.
Summary: On their daring trip to Valhalla, three Vikings, even the littlest, use their skills in different ways.
Identifiers: LCCN 2018020974 | ISBN 9781627796019 (hardcover)
Subjects: | CYAC: Vikings—Fiction. | Individuality—Fiction. | Size—Fiction.
Classification: LCC PZ7.A91178 Th 2019 | DDC [E]—dc23
LC record available at https://lccn.loc.gov/2018020974

Our books may be purchased in bulk for promotional, educational, or business use.
Please contact your local bookseller or the Macmillan Corporate and Premium Sales Department
at (800) 221-7945 ext. 5442 or by e-mail at MacmillanSpecialMarkets@macmillan.com.

First edition, 2019 · Design by Adam Auerbach and Carol Ly
The artist used pen and ink, watercolor, and digital color to create the illustrations for this book.
Printed in China by Toppan Leefung Printing Ltd., Dongguan City, Guangdong Province
1 3 5 7 9 10 8 6 4 2

THE THREE VIKINGS

ADAM AUERBACH

Christy Ottaviano Books

HENRY HOLT AND COMPANY · NEW YORK

Three Vikings were sitting around a campfire.

The littlest one was singing about Valhalla, the magical place where the strongest and bravest Vikings go. He sang of Valhalla's never-ending feasts, the golden tree that grows outside its doors, and the magical goat that nibbles the golden branches.

"One day I will be invited to Valhalla," said the first Viking,
"because I am the strongest."
"Yes you are," said the others.

"One day I will be invited to Valhalla," said the second Viking,
"because I am the bravest."
"Yes you are," said the others.

"One day I, too, will be invited to Valhalla," said the littlest Viking. The two other Vikings didn't say a word.

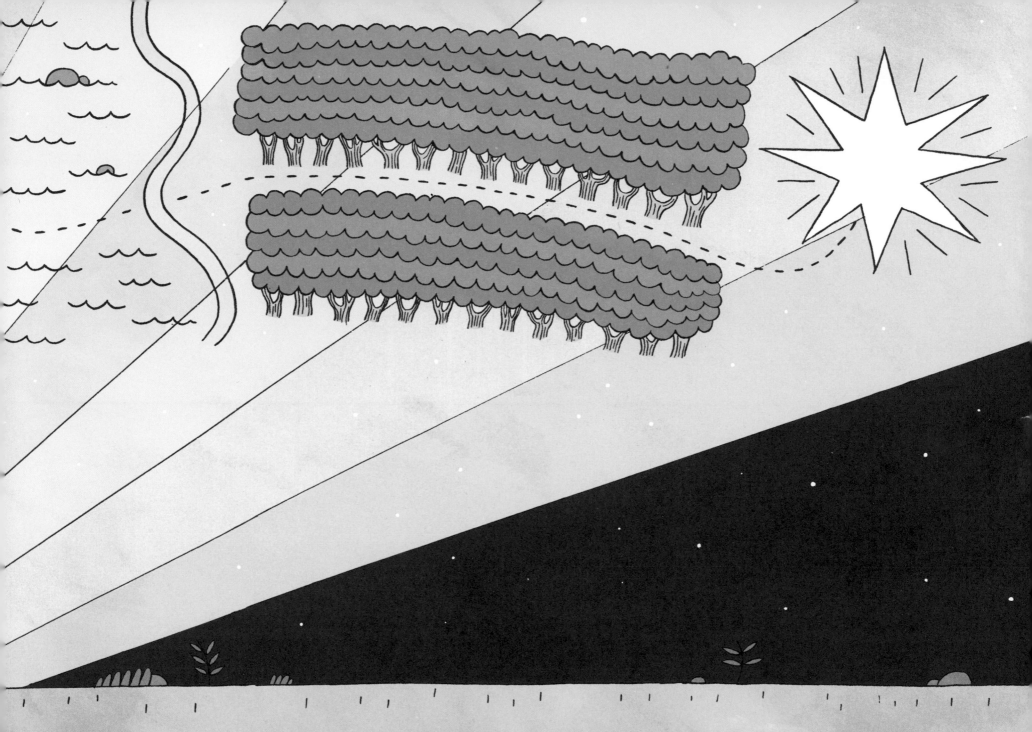

That night, all three Vikings dreamed that they were summoned to Valhalla. To get there, they had to travel over the tallest mountains, across the widest sea, and through the darkest forest.

They set off the next morning, but when they reached the tallest mountains, they came upon an ornery troll.

"No need to worry," said the little Viking. He began to sing a calming song . . .

. . . but the troll was not interested in music.

Luckily, the strongest Viking was able to give
the troll a lift back to where he belonged.

"Thanks," said the little Viking, "but if
there's any more trouble, I'll take care of it."
The two other Vikings did not reply.

While sailing over the widest sea, the Vikings ran into trouble again.

"Let me handle this," said the little Viking. He began to sing a lullaby . . .

. . . but the kraken would not go to sleep.

Luckily, the bravest Viking was there to help.

"Thanks," said the little Viking, "but next time I've got it covered."
The two other Vikings remained silent.

Deep in the darkest forest, the Vikings bumped
into a fire-breathing dragon.

"Stand back, everyone," said the little Viking.
He began to play his wildest dance tune.

The dragon loved the song—

but decided that she wanted the little Viking's instrument
for herself. The two other Vikings gave up their shields
so that their friend could keep his lyre . . .

. . . and the dragon could make some music of her own.

"Thank you very much," said the little Viking.

"Next time I'll be able to help, right?"

"Maybe you should just leave things to us,"
said the other two.

After traveling for what felt like years, the three Vikings finally arrived at Valhalla.

"I knew I would make it here, because I'm the strongest," said the first Viking.

"I knew I would make it here, because I'm the bravest," said the second.

"But why am I here?" asked the little Viking.

The two other Vikings didn't know what to say.

When the three Vikings entered the grand hall at Valhalla,
they were greeted by a cheering crowd. Once everyone saw the
little Viking's lyre, they called out for him to sing. Valhalla was
full of strong and brave Vikings, but none of them were musicians.

They had been waiting for just the right Viking to come
along and fill their days with music and stories.

"This is the song of three Vikings and their journey
to Valhalla," the little Viking said.

Then he began to play his lyre and sing.

At last, the little Viking was happy to be helpful.